Little Mole's Christmas Gift

by Glenys Nellist
illustrated by Sally Garland

beaming ☀ books

MINNEAPOLIS

For James, one of life's most precious gifts to me.
I love you, Mum. —G.N.

For Johnny and Ron. —S.G.

Text copyright ©2020 Glenys Nellist

Illustrations copyright ©2020 Beaming Books

Published in 2020 by Beaming Books, an imprint of 1517 Media.
All rights reserved. No part of this book may be reproduced
without the written permission of the publisher.
Email copyright@1517.media. Printed in Canada.

26 25 24 23 22 21 20   1 2 3 4 5 6 7 8

ISBN: 978-1-5064-4875-6
Ebook ISBN: 978-1-5064-6654-5

Library of Congress Cataloging-in-Publication Data

Names: Nellist, Glenys, 1959- author. | Garland, Sally Anne, illustrator.
Title: Little Mole's Christmas gift / by Glenys Nellist ; illustrated by Sally
  Garland.
Description: Minneapolis, MN : Beaming Books, [2020] | Series: Little Mole
  | Audience: Ages 5-8. | Audience: Grades K-1. | Summary: While bringing
  home the perfect Christmas gift for his mother, the most beautiful
  mushroom he has ever seen, Little Mole encounters woodland friends in
  need and shares the mushroom with them.
Identifiers: LCCN 2019056257 (print) | LCCN 2019056258 (ebook) | ISBN
  9781506448756 (hardcover) | ISBN 9781506466545 (ebook)
Subjects: CYAC: Kindness--Fiction. | Gifts--Fiction. | Christmas--Fiction.
  | Moles (Animals)--Fiction. | Forest animals--Fiction.
Classification: LCC PZ7.1.N433 Ljm 2020 (print) | LCC PZ7.1.N433 (ebook)
  | DDC [E]--dc23
LC record available at https://lccn.loc.gov/2019056257
LC ebook record available at https://lccn.loc.gov/2019056258

VN0004589; 9781506448756; AUG2020

Beaming Books
510 Marquette Avenue
Minneapolis, MN 55402

Beamingbooks.com

It was going to be the best Christmas ever.
Little Mole had found the perfect gift for Mama.
It was the biggest, the best, the most beautiful
mushroom he had ever seen!

Little Mole leapt from the burrow
and scurried off through the snow.

There it was—his lovely mushroom, standing proudly above the rest. It was the biggest, the most beautiful, and definitely the best of the bunch.

Little Mole scampered
over in delight
and tugged.

But the mushroom
was stuck firm.

Little Mole scurried around
the back and pushed.

But the mushroom
would not budge.

Little Mole ran to the side and pulled with all his Little Mole might—until at last the mushroom creaked, and cracked, and toppled to the ground.

Little Mole clapped his paws in delight. Mama would be so surprised and pleased with Little Mole's big gift. Little Mole got hold of the mushroom and began to drag it through the snow.

But all of a sudden, he heard someone crying.

Who was that?

Little Squirrel was curled in a ball, holding her tummy with her paws.
"Little Squirrel, whatever is wrong?" Little Mole asked.

"Oh, Little Mole," the squirrel cried, "I haven't eaten all day!
I'm so hungry!"

Little Mole looked at his mushroom. He looked at Little Squirrel. Maybe he could break a piece off the stem—it would still make a lovely, big gift for Mama. And so Little Mole broke off some of the stem and gave it to Little Squirrel.

"Thanks, Little Mole. You are so kind!" Little Squirrel said as she munched on the mushroom.

Little Mole was nearly home when he heard someone whimpering. Who was that?

Little Mouse was lying on his side, curled up by a rock. "Little Mouse, whatever is wrong?" Little Mole asked.

"Oh, Little Mole," the mouse cried,
"I haven't slept all day! Little Weasel
stole my pillow, and I'm so tired."

Little Mole looked at his mushroom.
It was nice and soft. It would make
a good pillow. He looked at Little
Mouse. Maybe he could break off
another piece of the stem—it would
still be a lovely, big gift for Mama.

And so Little Mole broke off some of the stem and gave it to Little Mouse.

"Thanks, Little Mole. You are so kind!" Little Mouse said as he snuggled in for a nap.

Little Mole was just in sight of his burrow when
he heard someone sobbing. Who was that?

Little Chipmunk was shivering, looking up fearfully
at the dark clouds. "Little Chipmunk, whatever is wrong?"
Little Mole asked.

"Oh, Little Mole," the chipmunk cried, "I'm so scared
of the winter storm, and I have a long trip home.
If only I had an umbrella to protect me."

Little Mole looked at his mushroom. He looked
at Little Chipmunk. The top of his mushroom would
make a perfect umbrella. But if he gave it away,
he wouldn't have a big gift for Mama anymore.

Little Mole didn't know what to do.

Just then, icy rain started to fall. Little Chipmunk
covered her head with her paws and closed her eyes.

Quickly, Little Mole broke off the top of the mushroom
and gave it to Little Chipmunk.

"Thanks, Little Mole. You are so kind!" Little Chipmunk said as she took shelter under the mushroom.

Back in the burrow, Little Mole
looked sadly at his little gift.
It wasn't the big gift he'd hoped for.

"Merry Christmas, Mama," Little Mole said
quietly as he handed his present to her.

"Little Mole," she said as she unwrapped her gift,
"what a wonderful mushroom!
This will make a delicious soup
for our Christmas supper!"

Little Mole sniffed.
"I suppose so,
Mama," he said.

"Whatever is wrong,
Little Mole?" Mama asked.

"It used to be a big beautiful
mushroom, Mama. The best
one in the forest," Little Mole
explained. "But I gave
most of it away to friends
who needed it."